The Pink Dolphin

By Thomas McDermott-Post
in collaboration with Mayor Billy Keyserling

Illustrated by Bill Dula

THE FIG & THE VINE
PUBLISHING, LLC

About Our Little Book

Not long ago, while sitting on a swing at the local waterfront park, soaking up the warm sun and the cool sea breezes coming across the beautiful Beaufort River, I was thinking about what an honor and responsibility it is to be the Mayor of my own hometown, Beaufort, one of the most historic cities in the country.

I was also pondering the challenges of leading the City Council and our community through the largest financial crisis of our generation. The part of my new job I did not anticipate when I ran for Mayor was how to inspire people to understand a need for their government to work differently from the way it has operated in the past. How to embrace, rather than fight, change.

Suddenly, I felt a gentle tap on my shoulder and saw my friend Thomas, an eight year old and a very wise young man, standing at my side. We began talking and in terms I hoped a third grader could grasp, I explained to Thomas the need for all of us to work together through the financial storm and into an uncertain future. I told him my challenge was to inspire a community that would either fight the changes or pull together to work through them. Thomas nodded and gradually our conversation turned to a boat passing by or a bird flying above.

A few days later, Thomas's answer to my questions arrived over the internet via email. It appears Thomas got my point and wrote the following story which helped me, and hopefully others who read it, to understand how we must move forward to face the challenges and opportunities that lie ahead.

Billy Keyserling
Mayor of Beaufort, South Carolina

"In my 1986 novel *The Prince of Tides*, I wrote about a white porpoise that I saw twice as I crossed the bridge that led to Harbor Island. I was a senior at Beaufort High School and the sightings had a magical, nearly sacred, feel to them…The nine year old writer, Thomas McDermott, returns to this theme in his charming new book *The Pink Dolphin*. The magic's still there…"

—Pat Conroy, Author of *Prince of Tides*

"*The Pink Dolphin* appears to be a book for children. It's much, much more than that. This lovely, inspiring little book addresses the current divisive national climate that makes it so hard for America to accomplish anything in all our interests–and to unite in bringing us together for the good of all. Beautifully illustrated, and written with a simple eloquence, it's a book for all Americans at a critical moment for the country. Read it and be inspired too…"

—Haynes Johnson, Pulitzer Prize winning journalist and best-selling author

"*The Pink Dolphin* is a timely reminder to all of us of the value of cooperation and understanding. These qualities can produce miracles even when troubles loom and threaten. *The Pink Dolphin* is a captivating protagonist who teaches a universal lesson. Congratulations to Tom, Billy and Bill for a special book that will entertain and teach people of all ages."

—Joseph P. Riley, Jr., Mayor of Charleston, SC

"Simply rendered, beautifully illustrated, and delightfully entertaining, we discover anew that the world beyond ourselves enriches our own, that helping another helps ourselves and our community, and that in unity there is strength. True to itself, it's a spirited collaborative work which celebrates the spirit of collaboration…"

—Bernard M. Schein, Author of *If Holden Caulfield Were in My Classroom*

"This is a beautiful story with a child's clear message. We adults can learn so much from our children. *The Pink Dolphin* teaches us that our communities are better and stronger when we all respect each other and work together for the benefit of all."

—Richard Riley, Former Secretary, U.S. Department of Education, Former Governor, SC

The Pink Dolphin

A Tale of Working Together

By Thomas McDermott-Post
in collaboration with Mayor Billy Keyserling

Illustrated by Bill Dula

2

*O*nce upon a time, in a pretty, historic little town called Beaufort, a really amazing thing happened! Now, this little town sat on the banks of a big, wide river that flowed right into the ocean. In this river, bottlenose dolphins lived and humans fished and caught shrimp.

The town was very special – almost magical. And the dolphins were very special, too. They were beautiful colors, violet, green, blue, and yellow. And there was one pink dolphin. Only one. She was different from the rest, and always full of plans.

*B*ecause she was different, the other dolphins sometimes laughed at her and made fun of her big ideas. This dolphin often spent time alone, swimming through the creeks and rivers by herself.

*O*ne of her favorite things to do was to follow the shrimp boats. Unlike many of her fellow dolphins, she liked people and boats, and the shrimpers liked her, too. They thought of the strange pink dolphin as a good luck sign. When they would see her, they would throw part of their day's catch to her as a thank you for bringing them a safe day on the water.

*S*he tried to tell the other dolphins in her pod about the wonderful meals that the shrimpers gave her, but they all laughed at her and told her that dolphins and humans don't work together.

"It's been tried," they said. "It just doesn't work. If you get too close to the humans, you'll just get caught up in their nets – they are trouble and it's just not worth it."

*O*ne hot August day, the dolphins felt that something was different in the water. When they surfaced, they saw the skies were overcast and threatening, and all the sea creatures were nervous. A terrible storm was coming! The dolphins knew that when the storm hit, the seas would be dangerously rough, and food would be hard to find. They set out to gather as much food as they could, and then they sought shelter in the deep, safe water.

But the pink dolphin worried about her human friends, the shrimpers, and she begged her pod mates to help her find their boats and warn them about the coming storm.

"No," said the other dolphins, "we have to stay in the deep water and the humans will have to take care of themselves. Soon food will be scarce and the rivers will be dangerous!"

So the pink dolphin set out on her own to help her friends, the shrimpers. She swam as hard and as fast as she could through the rivers, and as she found each boat, she leapt out of the water into the air, over and over again, until the busy shrimpers noticed her strange behavior. When they looked up at her, they noticed the threatening sky and decided to head in to the docks.

*B*ut one boat was still missing, and the dolphin continued on, although there was so much water to search and she was getting very tired and feeling frightened.

Finally, right when the storm hit, she could see the last boat up ahead, stranded on a sandbar where it had been pushed by the strong currents and wind! The boat was heavy with the day's catch, and the crew had been pitched overboard when the boat ran aground. The shrimpers were in for a hard time.

*T*he pink dolphin knew she could not save everyone by herself. There were too many people who needed help and they needed it soon or they would be drowned! She quickly ducked under water and sent out a powerful call for help, her own personal signature whistle. No one answered. She tried again. No answer.

She understood why her fellow dolphins were not answering her call. Because they did not want to help the people. She knew their excuses. The people were not their kind, let them take care of themselves, the waters were too dangerous... But she refused to give up. She began another call, first her special whistle and then an urgent plea of clicks in her dolphin sonar.

"We all live here together! We all depend on these waters for our food and our lives! Perhaps if we help them, they will someday help us!"

At first she heard nothing. She swam to each shrimper struggling in the water and tried to push him to the diminishing sandbar, but the waters were churning and strong, even for her powerful body and there were more men in the water to be saved.

What she didn't know was that the dolphins in her pod were feeling bad. It seemed so lonesome without her. They could hear her pleas. Although safe in the deep, they could imagine the horrible current fighting against their friend.

"She must be frightened!" exclaimed the blue dolphin. "She will be hurt!" cried the violet dolphin. "Oh, those horrible people!" raged the orange dolphin. "It's not their fault – they can't help being people and they didn't make this storm!" huffed the green dolphin. "And I bet they are as scared as she is! And what if we DO need their help one day?" he added.

They swam slowly in a circle, each thinking about their friend and the humans in danger. All at once they all knew what to do. "Right. Let's go!" decided the orange dolphin. Off they swept, racing through the raging current towards the sound of their friend.

The pink dolphin rejoiced to see her colorful friends appear out of the gloomy darkness underwater. There were only a few of them but they each had a talent. The green dolphin was very strong and could push. The blue dolphin was very kind, and could comfort the frightened shrimpers. The orange dolphin could organize the rescue effort.

While there weren't many of them, the dolphins found that by using their talents and working together, they were able to help the men back on the boat and keep the vessel safe in the shallow water until the storm subsided.

17

As the skies cleared, the grateful shrimpers rushed to help the pink dolphin, feeding her as much as she could eat, and expressing their thanks. They fed the rest of the pod, too, and suddenly, they saw before them a rainbow of dolphins. The humans felt so lucky and the dolphins felt so proud, that a bond was formed that very moment that could never be broken.

*T*o this day, you can watch pods of dolphins following the shrimp boats in the Beaufort River. And seeing a pink dolphin is still considered good luck!

The development of *The Pink Dolphin*, a "collaboration about collaboration," is brought to you by an eight year old student, a 61 year old small City Mayor and an 83 year young illustrator.

The primary author, Thomas McDermott-Post, was 8 years old when he wrote this book with Mayor Billy. Thomas enjoys reading, movies, and art. He would like to be an archeologist or an actor when he grows up. A native Beaufortonian, he is active in his community and takes a great interest in the challenges that face his family, friends, and neighbors. He hopes that this book will remind us all of the need to appreciate our differences and the strength we can have when we all work together.

The illustrator, Bill Dula, was born, and for the most part, raised and educated in New York City. Following his illustrious career as an illustrator, Bill and his wife Marie retired to Beaufort, where Bill continues to paint and draw, winning awards for his art. His 50 plus year career included assignments with many prestigious publishers, and a contract with NBC TV for whom he created hundreds of illustrations for The Huntley-Brinkley Report and The Nightly News among other assignments. Bill is a member of the Society of Illustrators and has been published in their Annuals. His works have been featured in many galleries, museums, and publications. Bill's talents were also employed as a courtroom sketch artist.

The instigator and collaborator of this tale, Billy Keyserling, had a grandfather who arrived in Beaufort, South Carolina in 1888, after fleeing Tsarist Russia. Since then, Keyserlings have been leaders in the community, running successful businesses, providing healthcare for the less fortunate, and serving in elected positions from the County Council to the SC House of Representatives. After a career working on and around Capital Hill in Washington, DC, Billy returned home where he served in the State Legislature, on Beaufort City Council, and in many community and civic organizations. Billy was elected Mayor of Beaufort in 2008. With a challenging economic climate and a changing city, Billy is excited to continue the family legacy of public service and to help the city of Beaufort work with its citizens to preserve a sense of community and cooperation for Beaufort's future.

9 780984 108701